The real Farmer in the Dell

written by Sandra Sutter

illustrations by

Chantelle and Burgen Thorne

The Farmer in the Dell

The far - mer in the dell. The far - mer in the dell.

Heigh Ho the der - ry O! The far - mer in the dell.

Verse 1:
The farmer in the dell.
The farmer in the dell.
Heigh Ho the derry O!
The farmer in the dell.

Verse 2:
The farmer takes a wife.
The farmer takes a wife.
Heigh ho, the derry O!
The farmer takes a wife.

Verse 3:
The wife takes a child.
The wife takes a child.
Heigh ho, the derry O!
The wife takes a child.

Verse 4:
The child takes a dog.
The child takes a dog.
Heigh ho, the derry O!
The child takes a dog.

Verse 5:
The dog takes a cat.
The dog takes a cat.
Heigh ho, the derry O!
The dog takes a cat.

Verse 6:
The cat takes a mouse.
The cat takes a mouse.
Heigh ho, the derry O!
The cat takes a mouse.

Verse 7:
The mouse takes the cheese.
The mouse takes the cheese.
Heigh ho, the derry O!
The mouse takes the cheese.

Verse 8:
The cheese stands alone.
The cheese stands alone.
Heigh ho, the derry O!
The cheese stands alone.

The real Farmer in the Dell

written by Sandra Sutter

illustrations by Chantelle and Burgen Thorne

The far - mer in the dell.

The farmer in the dell.
The farmer in the dell.
Hi-ho the . . . WAIT! STOP!

This song is all wrong!
I know because I was there.

The farmer didn't live in a dell.

rancher

The ~~farmer~~ lived out west on a RANCH!

Like this!

The rancher on the range.
The rancher on the range.
Off to the rodeo,
the rancher on the range.

rancher

The farmer took a wife

The rancher took a wife.
The rancher took a wife . . .
NOW WAIT A MINUTE!

The rancher didn't take a wife.
She took a HUSBAND!

The rancher took a husband.
The rancher took a husband.
Off to the rodeo,
the rancher took a husband.

Now, the husband did NOT take a child.
No way!
He learned to run a chuck wagon.

Like this!

The husband learned to help.
The husband learned to help.
Off to the rodeo,
the husband learned to help.

The next part IS mostly true.
When the rancher had a child,
the child took a dog.

Or three.
Maybe four.

The child took some dogs.
The child took some dogs.
Off to the rodeo, the child took some dogs.

The dogs took a cat.
The dogs took a cat . . . WOAH!
NOT SO FAST!

Dogs can't take cats anywhere.
Instead,
a stray cat showed up one day
and made herself at home.

Like this!

A cat came along.
A cat came along.
Off to the rodeo,
a cat came along.

The cat did take a mouse.
That part is true.
Poor guy.

When he finally got away,
he ran and ran
and never looked back.

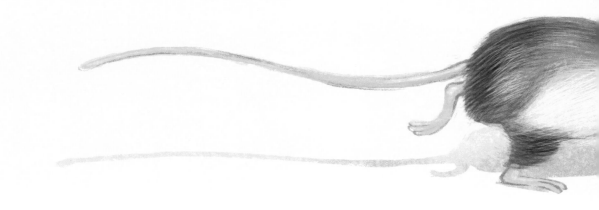

Like this!

The mouse got away.
The mouse got away.
Off to the rodeo, the mouse got away.

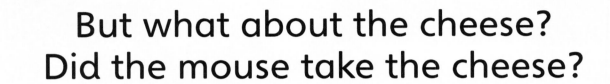

But what about the cheese?
Did the mouse take the cheese?

There it was.

Alone.

Unattended.

What was I to do?
What would YOU do?

Like this!

The cheese was up for grabs.
The cheese was up for grabs.

Mmmmm, mmmmm,
mmmm, mmmmm,
mmmm, mmmm,
the cheese was really good!

So that's the real story,
and I'm sticking to it!

The ~~The~~ real Farmer in the Dell

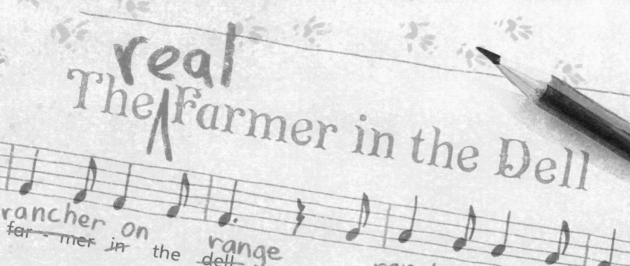

Verse 1:
rancher on the range
The ~~farmer in the dell.~~
rancher on the range
The ~~farmer in the dell.~~
~~Off to~~ rodeo
Heigh Ho the derry O!
rancher on the range
The ~~farmer in the dell.~~

Verse 2:
rancher ... husband
The ~~farmer~~ takes a ~~wife~~
rancher ... husband
The ~~farmer~~ takes a ~~wife.~~
~~Off to~~ rodeo
Heigh ho, the derry O!
rancher ... husband
The ~~farmer~~ takes a ~~wife.~~

Verse 3:
husband learned to help
The ~~wife takes a child.~~
husband learned to help
The ~~wife takes a child.~~
~~Off to~~ rodeo
Heigh ho, the derry O!
husband learned to help
The ~~wife takes a child.~~

Verse 4:
The child takes a dog. ✓
The child takes a dog. ✓
~~Off to~~ rodeo
Heigh ho, the derry O!
The child takes a dog. or two or three maybe four

Verse 5:
cat ... home
The dog takes a cat.
cat ... home
The dog takes a cat.
~~Off to~~ rodeo
Heigh ho, the derry O!
cat came along
The dog takes a cat.

Verse 6:
The cat takes a mouse. ✓
The cat takes a mouse. that's true
~~Off to~~ rodeo
Heigh ho, the derry O!
The cat takes a mouse. ✓

Verse 7:
got away yay!
The mouse takes the cheese.
got away yay!
The mouse takes the cheese.
~~Off to~~ rodeo
Heigh ho, the derry O!
ran and ran
The mouse takes the cheese.

Verse 8:
was left
The cheese stands alone.
was left not for long
The cheese stands alone.
~~Off to~~ rodeo
Heigh ho, the derry O!
was really good mmmm,
The cheese stands alone.
mmmm, mmmm, mmm.

For Wes, Mitch, and Olivia ~ Sandra Sutter

For Tommy and Tess, Bella and Rascal
~ Chantelle and Burgen Thorne

The Real Farmer in the Dell
Text Copyright © 2019 by Sandra Sutter
Art Copyright © 2019 by Chantelle and Burgen Thorne
Edited & Art Directed by Dr. Mira Reisberg www.childrensbookacademy.com

Summary: Everyone thinks they know the story of the Farmer in the Dell. But do they really? One little mouse knows the truth and he's ready to spill the beans. Take a seat in the saddle and hold on to your hat when you open the book and read all about it here. This real-life story will make you question what else might not be true, depending on who's doing the telling.

Clear Fork Publishing www.clearforkpublishing.com

P.O. Box 870 102 S. Swenson Stamford, Texas 79553 (325)773-5550

Printed and Bound in the United States of America.

ISBN - 978-1-946101-88-4

Sandra Sutter has worn many hats, including counselor, attorney, and now children's book author. She is also a wife, mother, and master finder of silver linings. Originally from the beautiful Front Range of Colorado, Sandra now lives in the heart of horse country outside of Lexington, Kentucky. An active imagination and two young children give her plenty of inspiration to write stories, research fun facts, and chase new dreams. Find out more about her at www.sdsutter.com

Chantelle and Burgen Thorne are a pair of married illustrators, working in a mixture of traditional and digital media. 'The Real Farmer in the Dell' is their first book for Clear Fork and they are very excited - especially 'cos it has lots of animals in it! On meeting new people they take turns at answering 'what do you do for a living?' because they get such a kick out of saying 'we illustrate childrens' books'!

Pssst . . . Want to have some fun? Draw your own story on the white pages.

Visit www.sporkbooks.com to see more great kids books.

CPSIA information can be obtained at www.ICGtesting.com
Printed in the USA
LVIW011619220319
611552LV00014B/384